Wynken, Blynken,

And Nod

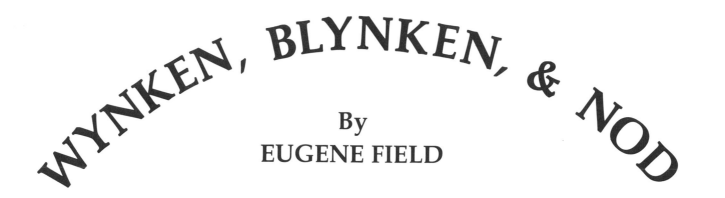

WYNKEN, BLYNKEN, & NOD

By
EUGENE FIELD

Illustrated by
HOLLY JOHNSON

Frederick Warne and Company, Inc.

New York and London

For Coit

Wynken, Blynken, and Nod one night
Sailed off in a wooden shoe —
Sailed on a river of crystal light,
Into a sea of dew.

"Where are you going, and what do you wish?"
The old moon asked the three.

"We have come to fish for the herring-fish
    That live in this beautiful sea;
Nets of silver and gold have we!"
    Said Wynken, Blynken, and Nod.

The old moon laughed and sang a song,
  As they rocked in the wooden shoe,

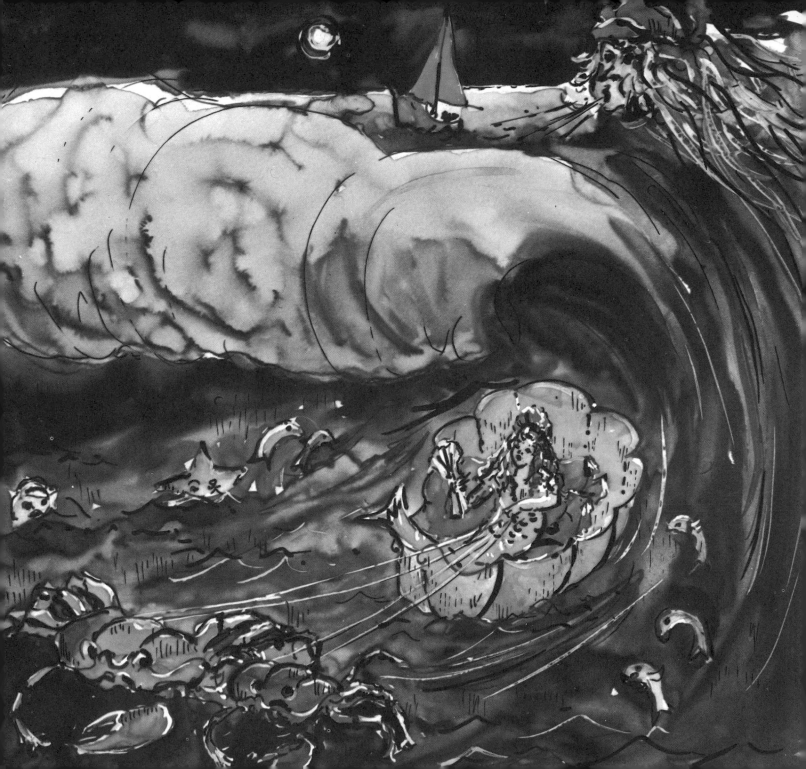

And the wind that sped them all night long
Ruffled the waves of dew.

The little stars were the herring-fish
    That lived in that beautiful sea—
"Now cast your nets wherever you wish—
    But never afeared are we!"
So cried the stars to the fishermen three;
    Wynken, Blynken, and Nod.

All night long their nets they threw
    To the stars in the twinkling foam—
Then down from the skies came the wooden shoe
    Bringing the fishermen home;

'Twas all so pretty a sail, it seemed
    As if it could not be,
And some folks thought 'twas a dream they dreamed
    Of sailing that beautiful sea —
But I shall name you the fishermen three;
    Wynken, Blynken, and Nod.

Wynken and Blynken are two little eyes,
  And Nod is a little head,
And the wooden shoe that sailed the skies
  Is a wee one's trundle-bed.

So shut your eyes while mother sings
Of wonderful sights that be,
And you shall see the beautiful things
As you rock on the misty sea,
Where the old shoe rocked the fishermen three;
Wynken, Blynken, and Nod.